WHEN LIFE GIVES YOU ORANGES

A RAINBOW CENTRAL STORY

ARIZONA TAPE

There's one thing Lisa loves more than anything and that's fruit. As owner of a small juice business, she attends a yearly food festival to share her passion with the world. But this time, she's not the only fruit fanatic on the block and the competition is about to get fierce. Who knew juice could be so exciting?

Reading suggestion: If you're easily influenced by descriptions of food, put some (orange) juice in the fridge before you start this story!

When Life Gives You Oranges is a F/F contemporary romance connected to the Rainbow Central series but can be read entirely on its own. It was previously named Her Juicy Lady and was part of the Eat Your Heart Out anthology.

CHAPTER ONE

"FRESH JUICE, get your fresh juice here! Freshly squeezed, delicious, healthy juice!" Erin shouted as she paraded back and forth our stall. She looked at me for reassurance and I gave her a thumbs up.

She continued her call for customers but most people passed us without a second look, already munching and crunching on much unhealthier options. A couple stopped in front of our booth, took their time to read the menu, but were tempted away by the delicious smell of the churros van further up ahead.

Dejected, Erin lowered her sign and joined me back behind our designated food festival tent. "Lisa! How are we doing?"

I glanced at the pile of oranges, mangos, and all

other kinds of fruit. For this time of the day, the heap was still way too massive.

Not wanting to kill the mood, I put on a smile. "Could be worse. Could be better. A lot better." I glared up at the cloudy sky. "If only the sun would cooperate."

Erin threw her towel onto the bar and cracked her neck. "Crazy that the weather influences so much."

"Like you wouldn't believe. Nothing convinces people to buy a fresh smoothie quicker than the threat of heatstroke."

"So you're taking advantage of their despair? That's evil," Erin teased as she leaned down on the bar.

"So is water in a bottle but hey. At least my juice is something you can't just do at home without a mess or fancy equipment. Unlike water which comes straight out of everyone's tap," I moaned as I finished cleaning one of the blenders. "Anyway. Thank you for helping me out. Can you believe my assistant is having a baby? Again?"

Erin grinned. "Well, it is nine months after kids go back to school."

"What? How's that relevant— Ewww. No. I don't want to think about her and her husband banging it out as soon as the school bus leaves. Why would you put that image in my head?"

"I merely suggested it. You're the one with the overactive imagination." Erin shrugged happily as she fiddled with a pink straw. "Anyway, glad to be here. I didn't have anything to do and you pay well."

"Anything for my best friend." I took another look at the crowd but the bad weather killed the potential of lots of customers. What a lousy first day.

Not expecting much sales soon, I sat down on the dingy fold up chair I brought. "How are your video projects going?"

Just the mention of videos made Erin beam. "Great. I'm working on something new. It's going to be fantastic. I hope."

"I'm sure it will be. I really liked Project Crush." I glanced back out, my eyes drawn to one of the stalls further down. The only other juice stand at the festival and from the looks of it, the weather wasn't harming them. "I wonder why they are so busy."

Making sure not to be too obvious, Erin snuck a quick look of her own. "They're not that much busier."

"Tssk. They weren't here last year. What kind of name is Her Juicy Lady anyway? That makes no sense."

Erin hummed. "Well… there's a lady selling juice so…"

"Yes, I know it does make sense. It just a stupid name."

"You're right. Fruit Friends is a much better name," my best friend reassured me as she gestured to the big banner behind us. "And at least you've got all those nice fruits on it. Hers is just a picture of some woman drinking from a straw."

I knew she was only saying this to make me feel better but it was hard not to compare stalls, brands, and amount of customers, with someone that was doing the same as me. If she could sell her juice on a rainy day, why couldn't I? What was wrong with my smoothies? Or what was so fantastic about theirs?

I pulled my apron off and shoved it under the bar. "Man the stall for a moment please? I'm going to check out the competition."

With my politest smile, I weaved through the crowd to the other juicy stall. The food festival was eclectic and there were so many competing smells and sights, but even from two booths away, the zing of orange caught my nose. They were lucky they weren't standing next to a churros stall.

I dug up a handful of coins and joined the queue. The two women in front of me had trouble choosing, giving me the perfect time to check out the menu and the people.

At first glance, the whole thing looked good. They only had one more person working their booth so they couldn't be much bigger than me. The blenders were from a brand I recognised and looked like they were kept clean. The fruit, while not as vibrant as mine, seemed fresh and fragrant.

The couple got their order and as they wandered off to the next stall, a teenaged boy smiled at me. "Hello, welcome to Her Juicy Lady. What can I get you?"

"What would you recommend?"

Before he could answer, a woman with short red hair appeared behind him and smiled. "Why don't you take your break? I'll handle this."

The teenager seemed confused but didn't hesitate long to jump on a break.

The redhead took his place, her smile never faltering. "So you're looking for a recommendation? What do you prefer, sweet or tangy?"

"Sweet."

"Berries or exotic?"

"Berries."

Her look intensified. "Juice or smoothie?"

"Either."

She flashed me a triumphant grin and pointed to

the big menu behind her. "Then I would recommend you the Cherry Berry Bingo. It's a smoothie with strawberries, raspberries, and cherries." As she leaned forward, her apron displaced and showed a glimpse of her cleavage. "Absolutely delicious."

"R-Right. I'll take that one then," I stammered, slightly taken off guard.

"Certainly." The woman turned away to gather the ingredients for the smoothie and skilfully cut them all up for the blender.

From the quick, precise cuts and her smooth, coordinated movements, it was easy to tell that she'd been doing this for a while. She looked a little younger than me but the skill was definitely there.

In no time, she placed two plastic cups in front of me and smiled. "There we go. One Cherry Berry Bingo and a Cucumber Fresh."

"I only ordered the one."

"The Cucumber Fresh is our bestseller. I figured you'd want to taste that one too when you go…" she clicked her tongue as she gestured to my booth. "Back to yours."

My ears burn hot. Awkward.

"Oh. So you recognised me, huh?" I mumbled, glancing at my stall where Erin hesitantly gave a hesitant wave, looking confused.

The woman chuckled as she held out her hand. "I noticed you earlier. I'm Julie, I'm the Juicy Lady."

"Lisa."

"Nice to meet you. Are you here for the full three days?"

I puffed up my chest. "Yes, this is our fourth year here."

"Wow. Nice. This is our first time. I guess you could teach us newcomers a thing or two." She glanced past me where a handful of people joined the line and smiled apologetically. "Sorry, I have more customers but I bet we'll see more of each other. Hope you enjoy your smoothies." She waved my attempt to pay away. "On the house."

With my two drinks in hand, I returned to my own stall, a little befuddled and unsettled

Erin grimaced and gestured to my face. "That bad?"

"Yes. I met Julie, the owner of Her Juicy Lady and she's very nice. She recognised me and gave me an extra drink. Both free of charge." I slurped from the Cherry Berry Bingo and groaned. "And this smoothie is freaking delicious. Ugh. So annoying."

"So annoying," Erin agreed as she took the other drink from my hand. "What's this?"

"I don't know. Cucumber something. Cucumber Fresh?"

My best friend slurped from the green beverage, her eyes widening. "Ooh, that's tasty. Definitely cucumber-y, definitely fresh. It's got some citrus in it, some mint. Really good."

"I hate vegetables in juices and smoothies. And what's the point of all those ridiculous names?" I grumbled while taking a reluctant sip. "Ooh."

"I know."

"That *is* delicious. I hate it."

CHAPTER TWO

WITH THE END of the first day in sight, Erin and I reluctantly started packing up our fruit and cleaning out some of our blenders. The poor weather had done a real number on our profit and I just wanted to get out of there.

Still, there was still about an hour of festival left and it seemed silly to leave when I could squeeze in a couple more sales. Despite my optimism, the thinning crowd didn't seem very interested.

From the corner of my eyes, I saw someone queuing up at our stall and I jumped up from my seat, only to recognise the redhead lining up. Julie. Probably here to scope out the competition.

She grinned from ear to ear once she caught my attention. "Hellooooo."

"Hellooo," I mimicked weakly, earning a muffled snort from Erin.

I didn't know what she was snorting about, I was actually a very bubbly and chipper person. Just not compared to the Juicy Lady who seemed to be all smiles, all the time.

"I came to check out the competition," Julie joked as she gestured to my juice list. "What's in the strawberry smoothie?"

"Strawberries and bananas," I replied dryly. "It's written under the name."

"Oh, so it is. I couldn't read it from over here." She cocked her head to the side. "So what's your bestseller? I bet it's the exotic smoothie."

"Actually, our bestseller is our orange juice. We're very well known for our orange juice," I corrected her, pride swelling in my chest. I didn't need fancy names and complicated drinks. My customers just liked their juice clean, fresh, and healthy.

Julie didn't seem phased. "Alright, I'll take one orange juice then. And I have to try the exotic smoothie as well. I love mangoes. It has mangoes, right?"

"Of course, it has the best mangoes in town," I replied. What kind of exotic smoothie would this be if it hadn't?

I turned around to Erin to call the order and let her make it while I remained in an awkward stare-off with Julie. Luckily, the loud rumbling of the blender and the chatter from the festival goers filled the tense silence.

"One orange juice and an exotic smoothie," Erin announced as she put the two cups in front of me. "That'll be—"

"It's on the house," I interrupted, pushing the two drinks forward with my best, brightest smile. "Enjoy."

"I'm sure I will," Julie replied cheerily, the sarcasm completely lost on her. She grabbed the cups and with a wink, she bounced back to her stall on the other side of the market.

She was barely out of earshot when Erin flashed me a smile. "So that was the Juicy Lady?"

"Don't start," I warned my best friend.

"She's cute."

I rolled my eyes. "I didn't notice."

"Come on, she's totally your type," Erin continued. "Bright, spunky, easy on the eyes. She even likes juice."

"Everyone likes juice."

"Not the way you like juice."

"Whatever." I glanced at the stall across the market where the redhead was slurping from her drink. "She's probably not even into women and besides, it doesn't matter. I'm not interested."

My best friend groaned loudly. "Come onnnn, it's been ages. You need to get over—"

"Nuh uh. We agreed not to say her name again. Ever. Whenever we talk about her, I run into her the next day. It's like summoning the devil," I said, shuddering. "It's creepy. Brrrr."

"Fine. But you need to get over the devil. Get back on the horse."

"No, thank you."

Demonstratively, I turned my back to Erin to stop the conversation about my love life. While it would be good to have someone to share things with again, it wasn't like Miss Right was just waiting around the corner.

With nothing to do, I grabbed a rag and gave the whole counter another wipe. Not that it needed it but I had to occupy myself somehow.

Luckily, two women with interlocked arms approached and gave me something to do. As always when I saw two women together, I wondered about their relationship. Partners? Lovers? Friends? Sisters? One of them looked a little older and was wearing a casual suit but that didn't help me determine anything.

"Hello! Anyone interested in speed dating?" The

girl around my age asked as she waved a stack of pinkish flyers around. "Speed dating for lesbians," she clarified as she handed me one of their flyers. "Well, women that are into women, really. Rainbow Central organises monthly events for people between twenty and thirty to mix and mingle."

I let out an awkward chuckle. "Yeah, I don't speed date."

"Why not? It's fun," the other woman said, the one in the suit.

Before I could reject their offer again, Erin popped up next to me.

"Quinn!" my best friend trumpeted.

They knew each other?

"Hey Erin." The younger woman gestured to me and the booth. "You're working here? No longer doing your films and video things?"

"No, I still am. I'm just helping out my best friend."

I gave a little wave, feeling a little awkward. "That's me. My employee had an unexpected baby so Erin is being a lifesaver and filling in for her. Hi, I'm Lisa."

The girl named Quinn chuckled. "Unexpected? She didn't know she was pregnant or it came out at an unexpected time?"

"Kind of both," I replied. "I think she was in a gas station buying snacks when her water broke."

"Oof," Olivia winced.

"This is her fourth baby in five years and they keep popping out at unfortunate times. She said this was the last baby two children ago. What kind of person winds up pregnant so many times by accident?" I asked rhetorically.

"Someone that doesn't like condoms?" Erin replied, not catching the rhetorical part of my question.

"Horny teenagers," Quinn quipped without missing a beat.

"Straight women," Olivia joked.

I snorted. "I don't think that's fair to straight women. Not all of them are obsessed with children."

The group nodded and murmured in agreement. I worried they'd continue the conversation, but luckily, Quinn pulled the focus back to her flyer.

"Are you sure you don't want to join the speed dating event?"

"Speed dating?" Erin squealed as she took the flyer from Quinn's hand. "Yesss!"

"Why are you so excited?" I questioned. "I thought you and Tasha were solid? Don't tell me there's trouble in paradise."

"No trouble. I'm excited for you. This is *exactly*

what I was talking about. Getting back on the horse. You *have* to go."

I pulled a face. "I don't want to."

"Come on! I..." Erin looked around and with a triumphant grin, grabbed one of the blenders. "I'll wash all the blenders for the rest of the event if you go."

"That's a tempting offer," I admitted. Washing blenders was the worst, even when using the soap and water trick.

Erin beamed as she turned back to Quinn and Olivia. "She's going."

"I didn't agree yet," I protested weakly. When it came to dating, a little encouragement was exactly what I needed and we both knew I was going to cave.

With a sigh, I snatched the flyer from Erin's hand. "Fine."

CHAPTER THREE

SPEED DATING WAS STUPID. It required people to make snap judgments about others and while I loved some snap judging, I didn't like when people did it to me. If that made me a hypocrite, it made me a hypocrite. At least I was self-aware.

I stared at the flyer, making sure the address was what I was standing in front. Not sure what to expect from a place that did speed dating for women into women, I was surprised to find a classic and rustic bar. Rainbow Central. That name was a little on the nose but I didn't mind it.

A little bell rang as I pushed through the glass door and stepped inside the cosy bar. At first glance, it looked classy and intimate. It certainly didn't have that kind of desperate vibe I always imagined about singles that came to this sort of thing.

One of the women that handed out the flyers earlier, the younger one, greeted me at the door. "Hello, welcome to Rainbow Central. Are you here for the speed dating?"

"I… guess I am."

"How lovely." She looked at me with piercing eyes and smiled. "Oh, aren't you Erin's friend? The one from the juice stall?"

"That's me."

"So glad you could make it. Lisa… was it? I loved your juice."

I smiled as I nodded. "Thank you. I… Sorry, I forgot your name."

"Quinn," she supplied. "Why don't you follow me? We're almost starting so can I get you a drink? On the house."

"I'll have a glass of white wine."

"Coming right up," Quinn said. "The event is through the red ropes, please sign in with Olivia over there."

Ah, the other woman from before. From what I gathered, they looked like they were in a relationship but I could be mistaken. There seemed a bit of an age difference so perhaps they were more like mother-sister or close friends. With women, it was always hard to tell.

I made my way over to the large barrel that

Olivia was using as her desk. She clicked a fancy pen demonstratively and hovered it above her clipboard. "Are you here to sign up for— oh, hey. You're the woman from the juice stall!"

She recognised me too? Apparently, I made quite an impression. Or maybe it was because I knew Erin?

Olivia shot me a smile. "How nice that you're here. Let me quickly explain the rules to you. It's a tenner to participate and includes two cocktails. You'll have five minutes to talk to each woman until we swap partners and we'll do two rounds so you get to talk to everyone twice. At the end of the night, if you'd like to make contact with another participant or participants, you can leave your details behind and you'll be put in contact if the feeling was mutual. We ask that you don't exchange any contact information during the date so nobody feels pressured into anything."

I nodded.

"During your blind dates, if someone makes you uncomfortable or behaves inappropriately, alert me or my partner, Quinn. Any questions?"

Only whether she meant partner romantically or in a business sense but that was just me being nosy.

I shook my head as I handed her a crumpled up bill. "Sounds good to me."

"Excellent. What was your name again? Lara?"

Maybe not so memorable then.

"Lisa," I corrected awkwardly.

"Great." Olivia jotted my name down on a sticker and handed it to me. "Please put that somewhere visible. I hope you have a good time."

I joined the group of people waiting around a couple of tables and chose to stand somewhere near the bar. Quinn handed me my glass of wine and I immediately took a sip, pleased to have something to do. If only I smoked, then I could wait outside without looking so awkward but I hated the taste.

I scanned the crowd to get a feel for the potential and the competition. One of the perks and cons of being surrounded by women with the same preference. Everyone was a potential match or a potential rival. Sometimes, quite often actually, both. It wasn't uncommon to date the ex of an ex.

At first glance, nobody really stood out to me. There was a good variety of women. Blondes, brunettes, redheads. Some with short hair, others in dresses, some with glasses, others with heavy boots. An eclectic mix of different tastes. Something for everyone.

After waiting for a couple of minutes, Quinn gathered everyone and led us further into the bar to a sectioned off area with small tables and chairs opposite of each other.

I zoned out while they explained the process again and the particular way they were organising the chair hopping to make sure everyone got to talk to everyone. Unlike with men and women, one side couldn't just remain seated. Everyone had to move at some point.

Confident I'd figure it out, I just sat down in my assigned seat and waited for the first date to show up.

A slightly chubby woman with very blue eyes took the chair across from me and folded her hands under her chin. "Hi!"

"Hey! I'm Lisa."

"Do you like cats?" she asked abruptly.

"Ummmm. I guess?"

"Awesome. They say you can tell so much by a person from their choice of pets. Personally, I have five cats. You could say I like..." she did a little drumroll on the table. "Pussy."

I chuckled awkwardly at her awful and cliché pun. "Five, Huh?"

"Yes. Do you have pets?"

"No."

"That's sad. Would you like to see pictures?"

Before I could answer, she shoved her phone in my face and flicked through a gallery's worth of cats.

"This is Pipi, my ginger beauty. She's the playful one, if you hadn't guessed. These rascals are Bayleaf and Thyme, they're two brothers I rescued. Aren't they cute? And then I have two more foster kittens, two striped tigers."

I nodded, not sure what was an appropriate compliment. "Yes… cute… whiskers."

"I know! I love their whiskers. They're so adorable."

She rambled on and on about her cats like somehow this meant anything to me and I was relieved to hear the bell.

"Aww, our time is already up," Cat-lady pouted. She hadn't even bothered to introduce herself.

"Such a shame," I lied, glad that the next person was already waiting to sit down. My relief was short lived.

I stared at the woman across, surprised to see her. "You."

"Hi! Lisa, was it? From the festival! I'm Julie."

"I remember."

"So funny that you're here too. I didn't realise you were… into women," she chatted as she sat down opposite of me.

"Well, I am."

"I would hope so. Otherwise you're in the wrong place." She sipped from the metal straw in her cocktail and shot me a beaming smile. "So. Where are you from?"

"Around here somewhere," I muttered. I really wasn't interested in dating the competition, especially not someone that liked fancy and complicated juices. Or worse, put vegetables in smoothies.

"How old are you?" Julie continued.

"Old enough."

"What do you like to do?"

"Things."

She raised her eyebrows. "Are you always this hostile?"

I faltered for just a moment. "Excuse me?"

"Look, you might be a really nice person, but right now, you're not being a very good blind date."

"That's because you don't know me," I defended myself. What an awful accusation.

"I'm trying to get to know you."

"I don't fraternise with the enemy."

The flickering candle on top of an empty glass bottle set a cosy atmosphere that really contrasted the tension hanging between us. Even if the whole place was set up for romance, I just wasn't feeling it. Especially not with Julie.

"Enemy?" She laughed as she played with her red hair. "What makes me the enemy?"

"We're in the same business. The festival really isn't big enough for *two* juice stalls and you're luring people with your flashy banner and Cherry berry Blasts or whatever," I scoffed, not managing to keep the bitter tone out of my voice.

"Bingo."

"What?"

Mischief sparkled in Julie's eyes. "Cherry Berry Bingo. Although Cherry Berry Blast has a good ring to it."

"So you have no problem dating the enemy?"

"Oh, come on, it's just some friendly competitions."

"Friendly competition?"

"Yes. So when was your last relationship?" she asked, pretending like nothing was going on.

I glanced around, trying to spot Quinn or Olivia. This probably didn't count as inappropriate behaviour but I just didn't want to chat to the woman that was directly affecting my profit.

When I couldn't get hold of either, I sighed. "Are we really doing this?"

"It's a dating event, isn't it?" She rolled her eyes slightly. "Anyway, you only have to put up with me for… three more minutes."

"Fine." Not wanting to be the one to ruin the night or start drama, I figured I'd just go along. "My last relationship ended a year ago. Yours?"

"About two years ago."

"What happened?"

Julie chuckled. "Is that really what you want to talk about on our first date?"

"You brought it up."

"What's your favourite fruit?" she asked, ignoring me.

"Strawberry."

"You?"

"Tomato." She laughed at my expression. "I'm kidding. I like oranges. My grandpa owned an orange orchard and we used to visit all the times when we were kids. Now I only get down there once or twice a year, but I never miss the prime season."

"I love orange orchards," I admitted reluctantly. "I think they're my second favourite fruit."

"Great second choice." Julie smiled. "I just love the smell and the way the juice explodes in your mouth."

"The tangy sweetness. There's nothing like it. When I was in high school, we took a trip to an orchard and got to see these fresh oranges. That's where I fell in love with it all."

"Is that why you got in the juice business?"

"Partially. I was also tired of paying a fortune for juice at the gym."

"And now you make other people pay you a fortune," she joked. "I'm kidding, your prices are actually really reasonable. Especially for the quality. I really enjoyed that exotic smoothie earlier."

"I really enjoyed your Cherry Berry *Blast*," I teased.

She chuckled. "Bingo."

"Cherry Berry Bingo," I repeated, finding myself smiling. "Now your Cucumber Fresh… While it was tasty, I just don't believe in vegetables in smoothies."

Julie's lips tugged up in a grin. "Oh, you're one of those people."

"What people?"

"Vegetable deniers."

Before I could argue more, the bell rang and cut the conversation short. To my surprise, I was reluctant to move away from Julie and wanted to talk more to her. Even if it was to continue the debate about vegetables, I had to admit… She was fun. What was wrong with me?

CHAPTER FOUR

While there was technically nothing wrong with the next set of dates, I found myself glancing at Julie and trying to figure out whether she was having a good time with her current date or not. From the laughter, it looked like she was hitting it off with pretty much everyone but she seemed like a pleasant person in general. It was probably just that.

Only particularly interested in the other woman across the table, I mostly nodded and hummed in response, only listening with half an ear.

"Lisa?"

Hearing my name snapped me out of my thoughts and the staring at Julie. "Yes?"

I looked up to an expectant face, probably waiting for an answer to a question I didn't hear.

Pretending it was the music, I cupped my ear. "Sorry, what did you ask?"

"What your idea of a perfect date is," the woman repeated. "I love a good old fashioned dinner with a movie."

"Oh, umm… A walk through an orchard," I said, thinking back to Julie. I wouldn't mind taking a stroll through an orange groove with her.

"That sounds fun, although I don't really eat fruit."

I stared at my current date. "Sorry?"

"I don't like many vegetables either, especially the green ones."

"O-kay… So what kind of dinner are you having on your perfect date?"

"Oh, like steak and potatoes or something meat-heavy. Lots of gravy, cream, butter. I know it's bad for me but I'll deal with that when I'm old," she laughed.

I wasn't very sad when the bell rang again and the meat-lover had to move on. While I had no problem with the occasional grease fest, I just couldn't imagine being with someone that didn't like vegetables. Or worse, fruit.

Bored, I waited for the next woman to show up but it looked like we were finished with the first round. Olivia and Quinn announced a small break before we had our second five minutes and I was more than happy to take a breather.

I ordered myself another wine at the bar, enjoying the slight tipsiness the alcohol was providing. It was nice to let my hair down and be out, even if this whole speed dating thing was a little tedious and not paying off. So far, I hadn't met anyone that caught my interest.

Well…

I glanced at the other side of the bar where Julie was chatting to the cat-lady. A slight twinge of jealousy shot through my chest and I decided to take my glass outside to get some fresh air.

At the door, the bouncer made me transfer my wine into a plastic cup before he let me out. With my drink in hand, I leaned against the front of Rainbow Central, taking in the night.

The bar was located close near the market where the festival was held and from here, I could almost see my stall. Midnight was only a couple of hours away so I should be able to catch enough sleep for what would hopefully be a better day tomorrow.

"Beautiful sky, isn't it?" a voice said to me.

I turned around and found myself looking at the redhead that had taken over my thoughts. "Hey, Julie."

"What are you doing out here? It's cold."

"I wanted some fresh air. And if I'm honest, a break from the ladies."

The redhead chuckled. "Nobody that caught your eye so far?"

"Not really. I just don't click easily with people. Most of my friends are people I've known for years from school or something."

"Ahh, close proximity. No choice but to make friends," Julie teased.

I shot her a slightly envious look. "Laugh. You're lucky you're one of life's pleasant people. Everyone likes you."

"Ah, everyone but you, apparently."

Her quip broke some of my frustration and I released a chuckle. "Apparently."

"Shall we go back inside? I think the break is almost over."

I groaned. "Do I have to?"

Julie laughed as she pulled on my arms and peeled me away from the window. "Yes! You never know, maybe Lindsay will turn out to be the one after all."

"Who is Lindsay?"

"The girl that has all the cats. Didn't she mention them to you?"

I snorted inappropriately loud. "Oh, she

mentioned them. It's not that I don't like cats, it's not what I want to talk about on a first date."

"What do you talk about on a first date? Let me guess, oranges," Julie joked.

She seemed in a very playful mood and I wondered if that was just her nature or if she was getting a kick out of teasing me. Maybe a little bit of both.

Surprisingly, I didn't seem to mind. In fact, it was fun to be around someone so lighthearted. Even if she was the enemy. Well… competition. And it wasn't like nobody ever got in bed with their competitor. In fact, it would be nice to spend time with someone that understood my passion for healthy juices and my love for fruit.

Except she loved embellishing and fancy names and vegetables in her smoothies. But those were just details…

Damn, I was starting to think like Erin. If she knew I was even considering it, she'd have a field day.

With a new drink in hand, Julie and I joined the other women for the second round. Small cliques had formed and there were a handful of pairs scattered around the sectioned area. Maybe the speed dating was a success for the others then.

I glanced at the redhead standing rather close to me. Well…

"I have to go to my place over there," Julie announced, gesturing to a seat a couple of tables ahead of mine. "I'll guess I'll see you in a turn or two."

"I look forward to it," I replied before I could stop myself.

Julie's eyes sparkled. "So you *are* having fun. Is it my endless charm that's doing it for you?"

I knew she was joking but she was undeniably charming.

"Just get to your table," I teased, giving her a gentle push.

"Alright, alright. No need to get violent with me," she joked, never taking her eyes off of me as she walked to her table.

She almost bumped into cat-lady and knocked off a drink, turning her smooth departure into an awkward but funny stumble. Still, I had to admit. It was charming.

With a smile stretching from ear to ear, I sat down at my designated table and tuned out the other woman, not able to keep my eye off of Julie. I didn't intend to be so tunnel-visioned and ignore the others, but I just wasn't done talking to her.

Every now and then, no matter who she was

talking to, she glanced at me and we shared a smile. My chest fluttered with a lightness that I hadn't felt in a long time.

Could it really be this simple?

After years of fighting and making-up with the devil, after leaving with a broken heart with all the love sapped out of it, could it be this simple to find something new?

I scoffed at my own naivety.

"Excuse me?" the woman across said, glaring at me.

Shit, I did that outloud. What did she think I was disagreeing with?

"So you don't think animals have a right to be slaughtered humanely? Wow. Wow!"

"No, I wasn't disagreeing with you! I believe in—"

"I just can't even," the woman interrupted, not letting me defend myself. She rose from her seat and waved at the front where Quinn was supervising the whole thing. "*Excuse me?* I want to report Lisa for hate speech."

"But I didn't say anything hateful!" I protested, my ears burning red when more heads turned towards us and the spectacle.

"You scoffed when I said that I don't eat veal or lamb and you were smiling when I described how pigs get slaughtered. That's so, like, cruel of you."

"I… I wasn't smiling at the pigs, I was smiling at *her*," I admitted, gesturing to Julie. "I promise I'm not pro animal cruelty. I don't even eat eggs from caged hens. This is all a mistake. I—"

"Ladies, let's not disturb the others," Quinn ordered, pulling us over to the bar. "Listen, everyone is entitled to their own opinions but we don't tolerate hate speech here."

"It was just a misunderstanding," I quickly said. "I promise I'm not pro animal cruelty."

"It sounded like it," the other woman scoffed.

"I'm sorry, it's not what I meant."

Quinn hummed as she tapped her chin. "Perhaps we'll just speed up the rotation, hmm? Would that be okay for you, Larissa?"

The other woman huffed. "Fine."

She stormed off, leaving me with a bewildered and exhausted Quinn. She looked at me. "You aren't actually pro animal cruelty, are you?"

"NO! Truth be told, I wasn't really listening. I… I was making eyes at someone," I admitted begrudgingly. It didn't make me sound good but I'd rather be inconsiderate than be accused of much worse things.

"Ahhh. I see." Quinn nodded as she rang the bell to indicate the round was over.

The room set in motion like a badly coordinated dance. People stumbled into others as they tried to make sure they were sitting with the right person next. Now that I wasn't part of the shuffling, I could enjoy the comical sight.

I waited until everyone had found their seats before I took place on the only empty chair in the room. I was met with a charming smile and my ears burned red. Of course, it had to be my turn with Julie.

CHAPTER FIVE

THE REDHEAD'S eyes twinkled mischievously as she folded her hands under her chin and leaned forward. "So… pro animal cruelty? Aren't you a catch."

"You heard that, huh?"

"I think everyone heard that," she teased.

"It's a good thing I have an early morning, otherwise I could have got hammered and I might have forgotten this humiliating event," I replied, the self-deprecation rolling off my tongue with ease.

Julie laughed. "Oh, don't you worry. You have me to help you remember tomorrow. Would you like the humiliation over a cup of coffee or tea?"

"Tea. I can't stand coffee."

"Animal and coffee hater? My, you've got some controversial opinions. I usually keep those for the third date but since we're being honest, I steal from the elderly and I believe the earth is flat," she joked.

I snorted and some wine shot up my nose. The liquid stung and travelled down my throat, making me choke on it. Caught in a coughing fit, I dove under the wooden table to avoid spraying my date with my germs.

A soothing hand rubbed over my back and I looked up to find Julie standing next to me, helping me not choke. The way she drew circles was soothing and the reassuring motion made me realise how much I enjoyed her touch.

Damn, this was not how this was supposed to go.

I sat up and shot her a smile. "I'm okay now."

"You sure?" she asked, concern wrinkling her forehead. She pushed a lock of red hair behind her ear before she gingerly touched my face.

The sudden intimacy started a burn behind my ears that travelled down my neck. As much as I could say I didn't want anything to do with my competition, it was clear another part of me didn't care about my objections. I wasn't even sure what it was about Julie that drew me to her like a moth to flame.

I cleared my throat and smiled. "I'm alright. Promise."

"Good." She lingered briefly, her thumb brushing down my cheek before she retreated and sat back down. "I'd much rather you didn't die during this date."

"Thanks."

She took a sip from her drink and winked at me from over the rim. "Although. Less competition tomorrow."

"Wow. You need me to die so you can sell more of your... Cherry Berry Blasts? Not much faith in your product, then," I teased.

"Bingo."

"Right, Bingo." I leaned forward, drawn in by the woman across me. "Okay, I have to ask. *Why* is it called Cherry Berry Bingo?"

"Do you really want to know?" Julie put her drink on a cardboard coaster and trailed her fingers down the glass, leaving streaks in the condensation. "The story is a little... Well, some people might think it's a little crass."

"Now I'm even more curious."

"Alright, so you know how sometimes women's..." Julie lowered her voice. "Breasts... get compared to fruit, right?"

I nodded.

She chuckled, her laugh slightly hoarse and sexy.

"Well… On a particular drunk occasion with my friends, we came up with Fruit Boob Bingo. We had a list of all kinds of fruit and if you saw a woman with a matching set, you got to cross it off. The rest is just regular Bingo."

I couldn't hold back my laugh. "That's awful."

"I know. We're awful when we're drunk."

"So out of curiosity, what kind of fruit was on the list?" I inquired.

"Well, obviously melons. Oranges. Apples. Pears. Cherries."

"Ouch."

Julie clicked her tongue. "Hey, don't underestimate the power of cherries. It's all about the nipples anyway."

I thought about her statement and found myself nodding in agreement. "Alright, that's fair."

"Well, I'm having fun," Julie declared. "Maybe you'd want to do this again?"

"I'm having fun too," I admitted. "But I have to think of my business. Dating the competitions… That'll hurt my profit margins."

"Better than a girl who hurts your heart."

"Ah, but what about someone that doesn't hurt either?"

Julie flipped her red hair back. "If you find a

woman like that, I'll change the name of my Cherry Berry Bingo smoothie."

"Oh yes? To what?"

"To Cherry Berry Blast, obviously."

I snorted. "You're funny."

"Which is why you should date me," she flirted. Her dark eyes smouldered as she reached across the table and brushed a finger over the top of my hand. "I think we'd have a lot of fun."

Despite knowing better, I didn't pull my hand away and instead, enjoyed the tingling sensation she elicited. Her feathery touch was light and no matter how much I wanted to deny it, made my chest flutter.

There was something about this woman… She was making me feel things I hadn't felt in a long time. Maybe it was just nice to be flirted with but it was more than that. I wanted to flirt back.

I watched her finger draw invisible circles on my skin and let myself enjoy the sensation. The candle light suddenly didn't seem so awful anymore. In fact, it only added to the surprising intimacy generated in less than five minutes. If she could set this mood during a speed date, who knew what she could do on a proper date.

No, I shouldn't be thinking things like that. I

really couldn't date her. It would only bring trouble and that was exactly what I was trying to avoid.

I pulled my hand back, immediately missing her touch. I pretended I didn't see the disappointment on her face and covered up my own with a big glug from my wine.

"So… Do you speed date a lot?" I asked between sips.

"No, not really. I'm mostly too busy but the festival is kind of like a holiday."

"But you're working?"

"Yes, but I'm also away from home and my shop. I have time carved out for relaxing and enjoying a good drink and meeting new, interesting people." She caught my eyes as she slowly drew out her sentence, the sparkle hard to resist. "You interest me."

I could feel my mouth going dry. "Why?"

"Why don't I explain that to you on a second date?" she suggested, waggling her eyebrows.

Before I could answer, the bell rang again and Julie got up from her seat. She leaned in across the table and for a moment, I thought she was going to kiss me.

Her lips inched closer but instead of making contact, moved past my cheek and to my ear. Her breath tickled the sensitive skin as she whispered. "I think we could have a lot of fun. Think about it, Lisa."

Only when she pulled away, I realised I'd stopped breathing. Damn. There was only half an hour left of the event before we were supposed to decide who we wanted to give our details to. When I first started, I didn't think I'd be interested in anyone but that decision had just become a lot harder.

CHAPTER SIX

THE NEXT MORNING, Erin was on me like a fly on honey. Blessed with having slept for more than five hours, she was buzzing with energy as she set up the stall in preparation of the day.

"And? And? How was it? Did you have fun? Did you meet someone?" she asked, bombarding me with her questions so fast, I didn't even have time to answer all of them.

"I didn't meet anyone," I mumbled, trying to keep the pounding in my skull at bay. With a heavy head, I stacked oranges in a tower near the front of the booth, hoping the vibrant colour would attract a lot of people. There weren't many clouds in the sky and the promise of sun and good weather would drive my business straight toward profit.

At least that was something to look forward to.

Spending the rest of the day with a sight hangover was not. I knew I shouldn't have had that last glass of wine, I was no longer a teenager, my body and liver were weak. I couldn't drink like I used to anymore, not even close.

A shadow fell over me and I looked up to find someone queuing.

"Sorry, we're not open yet," I announced before my fuzzy brain made sense of reality. "Oh. Julie?"

The chipper redhead popped a cardboard cup of tea in front of me and shot me one of her charming smiles. "Morning. Just reporting for humiliation reminder duty but I brought you tea."

I reached for the steaming beverage, touched that she remembered not to get me the standard coffee everyone had in the morning. "Thank you."

"You're welcome. That's my job done." She gestured to the colourful stall on the other side of the market where a thin guy was stacking kiwis and pineapples. Julie clicked her tongue and grinned. "Well, it's time for me to go back to mine. See you around?"

Afraid Erin would hear me, I nodded and kept my voice down. "See you around."

Julie was barely out of earshot or Erin was already hanging on my arm.

"I thought you said you didn't meet anyone!"

I shrugged my best friend off. "I didn't. We'd already met before the event, technically."

"Oh, pish posh and details. You two hit it off then?"

I looked in the direction of Julie's juice stall and hummed. "Sort of. It doesn't matter, she's going to be poaching our customers all day. Well, not on purpose but you know what I mean. We're fishing in the same pond here."

"Aren't we all," Erin snorted.

"Not the lesbian pond, the fruit juice pond!"

My best friend swung her arm over my shoulder and gestured up to the sky. "Come on, it's going to be beautifully blue today. There will be plenty of demand for fresh juice and smoothies today."

"You better be right," I said.

With Erin's help, I finished setting up the stall just in time for the festival to open for the second day. As expected from the sunny weather, the first visitors didn't keep us waiting long.

"Two orders of orange juice coming right up!" I shouted as I started the press and cut the oranges in pieces. The peel spritzed the fresh aroma through the stall and the smell of that sweet citrus was released as soon as the juices were pressed out of the halves.

I handed our first customers their cups of fresh

juice and watched as they took their first sip, relishing in the delight on their faces. There was nothing like fresh juice in the morning to get a great start to the day.

Unable to resist, I cut up some more oranges and pressed two more cups worth.

"For you," I said, handing Erin one.

My best friend didn't hesitate one moment as she took a sip from the paper straw. "Mmmm. So good."

I followed suit and let the fresh flavours dance on my tongue. Sweet, slightly tangy, a perfect taste of summer. I could taste the sun in my juice and just like that, I was no longer worried about profits or competition. The oranges spoke for themselves.

* * *

THE REST of the morning passed in a flash. The beautiful weather delivered plenty of thirsty people to my booth and the pile of oranges and other fruits was quickly declining. People were in a generous mood and couldn't resist spending their money, either on food or drink. It was a good day for every stall at the festival and I could feel the buzz in the air.

Whistling, I cut up more oranges and handed them to Erin for pressing. Despite her only helping out every now and then, she was really competent and if she wasn't so in love with her film making, I'd hire her permanently.

We worked seamlessly through the lunch rush, which was a little quieter for us than food stalls, and put a good dent in our fruit supply. With every sold cup of juice, my good mood grew and there was nothing that could ruin it.

I even hummed a little song while I was cleaning some of the blenders in the back. Even though technically Erin owed me for going on the speed dating, I wasn't going to hold her to it. It was my business after all.

"Oh oh," Erin muttered.

The first hint of dread circled up from my stomach as I rinsed the blades. "What?"

"The Juicy Lady… They're handing out samples."

I shrugged, not wanting to kill my good mood by worrying about Julie and her fancy smoothies. If they wanted to hand out samples, they could hand out samples. It was none of my concern.

"Good for them," I replied magnanimously as I shook the water off the tops of the blender. "I hope they have a great day. A fantastic day, even."

Erin let out a funny sound. "Yeahhh… but they're handing out samples in our zone."

"What?!" I rushed towards the front of our stall to see for myself. Julie was parading around the festival with a serving tray full of little cups of smoothies, which she handed out like candy. Which wouldn't be a problem if she wasn't doing it right in front of our stall. There was a reason our two booths were on opposite ends of the market and she was clearly violating the unspoken rule of sticking to our side.

She intercepted two women approaching my stall and handed them a sample, before directing them to the other side of the festival to her booth. So much for friendly competition. If that wasn't customer poaching, I didn't know what was.

If she thought I was going to let this slide, she had no idea who she was messing with.

I yanked off my apron and threw it on the counter. "Watch the stall for me."

"You got it," Erin mumbled, the worry clear in her voice.

She knew better than to stop me though.

I stormed through the people, heading directly for Julie and her tray of samples.

"Hey!" I shouted, spooking away a mother and a child. Whatever.

Julie directed her charming smile towards me. "Hello, Lisa. How nice to see you."

"No, it's not nice to see me. What do you think you're doing?"

"Handing out samples," she replied innocently

while presenting her tray to me. "Want one? I've got Cucumber Fresh, Lemon Zingers, and your favourite, Cherry Berry Bingo."

"You are unbelievable," I huffed. "Hand out samples in your own zone!"

"Zone?" She gestured around. "I don't see any zones."

"It's an unspoken rule, duh. Why do you think the two brownie stalls are on opposite ends? Or the two mead dealers? Direct competitors stick to their side. If you weren't first timers here at the festival, you'd know."

Only when I finished ranting, I realised I'd gone straight for the attack and never gave her the benefit of the doubt that perhaps, this was an honest mistake.

Even though her smile never faltered, the look in Julie's eyes changed. "Well, aren't you a doll for pointing that out."

Damn, I shouldn't have jumped to conclusions.

Before I could apologise, Julie flashed me a daring grin. "Well, there's only one reason you made a scene. Scared of a little competition, huh?"

I glared at her. "I'm not scared."

She chuckled as she handed out two more samples to passing people. "Well, then bite me."

"What?"

Julie turned away, her voice raised. "Fresh juice and smoothies! Get the *best* juice and smoothies at The Juicy Lady! Come and try some of our most popular flavours now!"

Ugh! So infuriating.

I stomped back to my booth, the plans brewing in my head. If she wanted to challenge me, it was on.

Erin read my mood before I even said a word. She held up a roll of plastic shot glasses and smirked. "I'm guessing we're handing out samples too?"

I flashed her a battle grin of my own. "You bet."

CHAPTER SEVEN

Not one to pass up a challenge, I was flat out exhausted by the end of the day. Between Erin and me, we'd handed out more samples than I could count and reduced our supply of fruit to a record low for day two.

While the festival was shutting down, we cleaned the stall and washed out the blenders in satisfied silence. My whole body ached from being on my feet and I could feel the effects of being out in the sun the whole day. Still, the muscle strain was rewarding and felt like an achievement. Even if I had no idea how much Julie and The Juicy Lady sold, it didn't matter. We ended up making a small fortune and that made us a winner. I wasn't even mad anymore.

Satisfied, I patted Erin on the back. "Well done today. We slayed."

"Yeah, we did."

"Go home and get some rest, I'll finish cleaning up. You've done plenty today."

"It was lots of fun," my best friend grinned as she threw her towel in the pile of dirty laundry and rinsed her hands. "Right, I'll see you tomorrow."

"Yup. Say hello to Tasha for me."

"Will do!" Erin called as she grabbed her bag and left the stall. "Byeee."

I gave her a little wave and returned to tidying up the rest of my things while I was still buzzing and had the energy. I knew that as soon as I sat down, I'd collapse and be useless for the rest of the evening.

Just as I was on my way out, a figure leaned over the counter with a big smile. "So how was your day?"

"Pretty fucking awesome," I admitted as I took off my apron and looked up at the redhead. She didn't seem mad anymore so perhaps she had a good day as well. "How was yours?"

Julie grinned. "Same. I enjoy some healthy competition." She caught my eyes and paused. "You want to get a drink?"

I stared at her, not sure if I was supposed to be flattered or annoyed. "You have some nerve handing out samples on our side and then asking me out for a drink."

"You're right…" She paused for a bit as she

chewed on her lip. "I wanted to apologise about that, I really didn't know about the sides thing."

"And I shouldn't have assumed you did. I'm sorry too," I admitted. We both made a mistake but I liked that she was mature enough to admit it. More than that, I liked that I felt I could admit my fault too.

We stared at each other for a moment, the silence filled with expectations. Just when I was going to say something, Julie spoke instead.

"Well, I guess I'll see you tomorrow then. Sorry, again." She shot me a warm smile and turned, ready to walk away.

"Wait, what about that drink?" I called after her.

Julie paused and looked back over her shoulder. "Sorry?"

"Didn't you want to go for a drink?"

The redhead looked slightly taken aback. "I thought… Yes, I'd love a drink."

"Perfect." I locked my stall and joined her on the other side of the counter. The warm evening created a nice, cosy atmosphere and even though the festival was over, there were still plenty of people about.

A big grin grew on Julie's face. "Where are we going?"

"Rainbow Central since it's across the road?" I proposed as I started walking in the direction of the bar, leaving the empty stalls and booths behind.

Julie matched my pace effortlessly and we fell in a comfortable rhythm as we crossed the street to the cosy bar. I opened the door and held it for her like a gentlewoman, earning an appreciative smile from her.

The bar was surprisingly busy but nothing out of the ordinary for a saturday evening. It was rather early so the atmosphere was tame and intimate, rather than wild and drunk.

We chose a table in the corner with a single candle and sat down on opposite sides of each other, reminiscent of the speed dating the night before.

"Well… Here we are," Julie declared, looking at me expectantly.

"Here we are," I repeated, feeling slightly awkward now we were sitting down together. The whole day, we'd been playing off of each other and letting the buzz guide us, but now it was painfully clear that we didn't know each other.

I grabbed the menu and hid behind it, trying to pick out a drink.

"What are you having?" Julie asked as she studied the list herself.

"Not white wine," I muttered, thinking back to the pinching headache it gave me this morning. "I did like the cocktails yesterday. Which one was it that we got?"

"I think it was the Rainbow Central cocktail. They were very tasty. I wouldn't mind another one of those."

With that decided, I shot a look around to see if I could catch a server so we could get our order taken. I was sure I'd feel more at ease with a drink in hand.

It was Quinn who came to our table with a little notebook. "Evening, ladies. What can I get you two?"

"I'll have the Rainbow Central cocktail," I ordered, putting the menu back in its little stand.

"Same," Julie replied, doing the same.

"Excellent." Quinn jotted down our order and examined us both. "Hey, weren't you two here last night?"

"Yes, we were," I confirmed. "I'm Lisa, Erin's friend?"

"Oh, right. From the juice stall." She tapped the pen against her chin. "We haven't released contact details from the speed dating yet. Did you two exchange numbers?"

Worried she was accusing us of breaking the rules, I quickly shook my head. "No, no. Julie is also working at the festival. We actually met before last night."

"Oh, I see. Well, I hope you have a good time then." Quinn smiled and flicked her notebook closed. "Two cocktails coming right up."

She strutted away, leaving me and Julie chuckling awkwardly.

"Did she think we broke the rules?" I whispered.

Julie laughed. "Definitely. Come to think of it, did you leave your details for me?"

"Did you?"

She raised an eyebrow. "I asked first."

"Ladies first."

"I insist."

"So do I."

She stared at me, the realisation dawning on her face. "You didn't leave your number for me, did you?"

I scoffed, taking aback by how sure she sounded. "I. I… No, I… didn't. I told you, I don't date my competition. Usually…"

"Right."

My cheeks burned hot. Unsure if she was insulted or hurt, I couldn't but apologise. "Sorry."

"No, it's fine."

The awkward tension hanging between us was given a brief respite when Quinn brought us our drinks. She placed two colourful cocktails with metal straws on coasters and wished us a good night.

"Cheers?" I proposed, holding up my glass.

"Cheers," Julie responded, clinking her cocktails against mine.

Not sure what else to say, I took a sip from my drink. The fruity taste was refreshing but I could tell it was probably made from frozen cherries.

I put the glass back on the coaster, watching it draw a ring into the cardboard. "This is good."

"Agreed. Not as good as my Cherry Berry Bingo, but very good."

I chuckled. "You sold a lot of those today?"

"Loooads. How did your juice go?"

"Flew off the shelves. I barely had time to press them, I was basically throwing oranges at people," I joked, realising she'd managed to dispel the stiff and awkward tension effortlessly.

She laughed. "It was a good day, huh? Got to love what the sun does for a business like ours."

"For sure."

She took another sip from her drink and looked at me from over the rim. "So… shall we get to know each other a bit better or are you going to be hostile again?"

"What do you want to know?"

Mischief danced in her twinkling eyes. "How old are you?"

I snorted. "Old enough. Which is twenty-six."

Julie hummed. "Nice. I turn twenty-eight this year. What do you like to do?"

"I like… running. Swimming. Watching a good

sob movie. And juice, obviously." Relaxed by the conversation, I got more comfortable in my seat and returned the question. "What about you?"

"I'm not much of a swimmer but I enjoy a good run, mostly because it gives me time to listen to music. I love listening to music and singing along."

"You a good singer?"

"Not at all. Unless you like listening to a dying cat."

"That happens to be my favourite sound," I joked.

She laughed out loud, almost choking on her drink. "You're funny."

I felt my cheeks heat up and leaned in closer. "Yeah?"

She brushed her hand along my cheek, drawing me in closer. "Oh, yes. Very…" She pressed a soft kiss on my lips, her mouth warm and soft. "Funny."

Despite the shortness, it was an intimate and wonderful kiss. I savoured the feelings it elicited from me, basking in the growing warmth in my stomach and the flutters in my chest. I hadn't been kissed in a long time. Too long.

Julie released a slow breath. "Was that alright? Not too soon?"

"Very…" This time, it was my turn to move closer and capture her lips. "Alright."

She chuckled, suddenly a little shy. "Better than alright, I hope."

"Much better," I reassured her. I didn't even have to lie or embellish, I could still feel the kiss sizzling on my lips, leaving me wanting more. Much more.

CHAPTER EIGHT

ONE DRINK easily became two and two was quickly followed by three. It was the fourth drink that was special. I was serving the fourth drink at my place.

I wasn't exactly sure how I went from not dating my competition to inviting her over to my house but life wasn't a straight-forward road. Sometimes, things just happened and I wanted this to happen.

"Sorry for the mess," I said as I handed her a glass of fresh orange juice. I'd offered her an alcoholic beverage but one look at the oranges in the fruit bowl had made up her mind.

She accepted the drink and immediately took a sip. "Ahh… There's nothing better than fresh juice."

I laughed as I put my glass against my lips. "I couldn't agree more."

"Mmmm…" She licked her lips, humming in appreciation. "I've been meaning to ask, are these Castillo oranges?"

Surprised, I looked at her. "They are… How did you know?"

"The taste."

"Wow, I've never met anyone that could tell oranges apart like that."

She chuckled as she took another sip. "I should know, I grew up with them. My grandfather would kill me if I couldn't recognise a Castillo orange."

"Your grandfather…" The pieces slowly clicked together. "Don't tell me your grandfather *owns* the Castillo orange grove. They're the best oranges in the world."

Julie beamed proudly. "Our family has been in the fruit business for a looong time."

"Wow. I'm…" I put my half-finished glass of juice down, too in shock to drink. "Wow."

Amused by my lack of words, she finished her juice and pulled me closer by my waist. She rested her hands on my hips, her eyes smouldering. "You want to talk oranges all night or want to do some squeezing of our own?"

I tried to hold my laugh. "I'm sorry?"

She snorted, triggering laughter in both of us. "I

don't know where that came from. Oh my goodness, please forget I said that. That was so cringe."

I didn't know if it was the alcohol or the moment but it felt like the funniest thing I'd ever heard. I buckled and laughed so hard, it hurt my stomach.

It wasn't until I had tears streaming down my cheeks that I managed to compose myself and pulled Julie into me. She had the biggest grin on her face as I kissed her, encouraged by the buzz.

I opened my mouth, deepening the kiss and she moaned against my lips. While the laughter still hung in the air, there was a seriousness to both of us that framed the importance of the moment. We were having fun and joking around, but this wasn't a joke.

Her hands ran along the small of my back, teasing the hem of my shirt up. With every passing second, the kiss intensified and sent sparks up and down my spine.

Even though I only just met her, she felt familiar. Her soft skin, the way our hands fitted together, the way her lips moved against mine. She tasted like oranges and smelled like summer, my two favourite things combined.

Eager to make the most of the moment, I trailed kisses down to her neck and inhaled her scent. I could tell she'd been working hard all day but I didn't mind. If anything, it turned me on more.

I pressed my lips on her sensitive skin, nipping at it, and then kissing it better. I could feel her moans rumble through her, feel her breathing shallow as she pressed herself harder into me.

"You have a bedroom somewhere?" she murmured, her hands threading through my hair.

"I'm sure we can find one," I teased, capturing her in another kiss.

With my hand on her waist, I guided her towards through my flat and into the hall leading to my bedroom. There weren't many good reasons to leave a perfectly fine glass of orange juice sitting out on the counter but a beautiful woman was definitely one of them.

The door shrieked softly as I kicked it open and we stumbled over the carpet, luckily landing on the bed. The mattress dipped from the weight but broke the fall.

With her body on top of me, her hair tickled my face and I giggled into the nape of her neck. She brushed the red locks back and captured me in another kiss, letting the joy bubble up in our chests.

I couldn't remember the last time there'd been so much laughter in my bedroom. And it's only going to get better from here.

* * *

I LAZILY TRACED invisible patterns on Julie's bare stomach, relishing in the afterglow. There was different strain in my muscles than from before and the two left me desperate for a hot shower or a good soak. But that involved getting up and the last thing I wanted, was to move away from the redhead.

"Mmmm," she hummed softly, her fingers playing with my hair. "That was… Mmm."

"Was that enough squeezing for you?" I joked, earning an embarrassed chuckle.

Julie pulled the sheets up to her face and snorted. "Shut up."

"You're so cute. Are you blushing?"

"You're teasing me."

I pressed a kiss on the back of her hand. "You seemed to like my teasing earlier."

Her satisfied smirk wiped the embarrassed look clean off. She stretched her limbs with the elegance of a cat and practically purred. "What time is it?"

I fished my phone from the sea of clothes to check. "Almost two."

"Oh wow… We took our sweet time." She rotated her shoulder and shook out her arm. "I'm going to feel that in the morning."

Her comment made me snicker as I waved my fingers of my dominant hand. "That makes two of us."

"Hey, question. Could I take a shower? I've been in a hotel for a couple of days now and I hate hotel showers," she asked as she rolled onto her side.

"Sure, the bathroom is through there. There are spare towels in the cabinet under the sink."

Julie yawned as she slipped out of the bed and stretched demonstratively. There was a confidence to her that had nothing to do with her beautiful body and lovely curves. It was the kind of confidence usually earned after sleeping with someone for a while and becoming used to each other's bodies and blinded to the imperfections. While we explored each other thoroughly, I was sure there'd be plenty more secrets to discover, for both of us. Still, that didn't stop her from parading naked through my room, seeming perfectly content.

I watched her leave, admiring the sway of her hips, not able to keep the smirk off my face. That was one fine woman.

Unable to stop smiling, I relaxed into my pillow when I heard the shower run. The first hints of sleep tugged on me but it seemed rude to not stay awake, at least until Julie was ready to leave... or climb back into bed. I didn't really mind.

Listening to the fall of the water only added to the drowsiness and I fought to keep my eyes open, barely managing. Caught between two worlds, I snoozed until the bathroom door opened and Julie rained droplets on my face.

"Hey!" I laughed, glad to be snapped out of sleep's grip. "Good shower?"

"Excellent, oh, that was so much better than the hotel. I honestly don't understand how they can get away with such terrible water pressure."

"People don't stay long enough for it to matter?" I suggested, pushing myself up from the bed and pulling Julie back down with me. There was an ease to her, a sense of familiarity I never had with strangers. Spending time with her was effortless and it made me hopeful that perhaps, life didn't have to be so lonely.

Julie squirmed out of my grip and rolled onto her stomach, the towel barely covering her. She propped her head up and looked at me, a remnant of a smile lingering on her face. "So…"

"Yes?"

"Shall I call a cab or…?"

I folded my arms under my head, weighing the options against each other. "I can call you a cab. Or you could stay and we can walk together to the festival in the morning."

"I suppose we are going to the same place," Julie thought out loud.

"Hmm-hmm."

"And you're sure you wouldn't mind?"

I gestured to the side of the bed she was in. "Plenty of space. And hotel beds suck even more than the showers."

The thought of having to return to her room seemed to sway Julie's mind as she settled into the bed. "Thank you."

"No problem. I'm going to turn off the light," I said, reaching out to the night lamp on my side. With a click, the darkness surrounded us and teased the sleep back to the surface. My eyes grew heavy as I listened to Julie's breathing, surprised by how comforting it was to share my bed with someone again. Maybe it was weird to find reassurance in the presence of someone that was a stranger mere days ago but the rhythmic breathing was a nice reminder that I wasn't alone. That even if this didn't work out, I was capable of moving on and putting myself out there. With my mind full of hopeful thoughts, I drifted off to sleep, eager to see what the morning would bring.

I turned on my side to look at Julie and despite the darkness, found her looking back at me. She smiled, her lips plump from being thoroughly kissed.

That didn't stop me from shuffling closer and

capturing her in one more kiss. I trailed my hand up her hip, letting it come to rest in hers. My heart pounded as I watched the other woman and for some reason, I felt certain Julie was going to be an important person in my life.

EPILOGUE

7 MONTHS later

THERE WAS nothing like waking up to the smell of oranges with a beautiful woman in the bed. I hummed into the pillow and pulled the sheets tighter, enjoying the rare morning that I got to wake up in an orange grove.

It was a dream come true.

I reached across to brush a stray lock of red hair out of Julie's face, accidentally waking her up.

"Mmmm... Is it morning already?" she murmured, rolling onto her side to face me.

"It's almost nine."

Julie jolted up, tossing the sheets back. "No! We overslept!"

She tried to rush out of the bed but I caught her by the wrist and pulled her back in. "Oh, come on. One snooze isn't going to hurt."

"It's harvest season, Lisa. Harvest season!" She bolted to the window and pulled the white curtains back, letting the sun into the room.

As she opened the window, a gust of wind wafted the fragrance of fresh oranges into my face and I inhaled the scent, letting it fill my nose. This was heaven.

Drawn in by the smell, I got up from the large bed and joined my girlfriend by the open window, pulling her into me for a brief moment. I wanted to savour our trip to the Castillo orchard and I wanted to savour her.

With my arms wrapped around her, I admired the sight. The sun was already high in the sky and cast a beautiful golden glow over the rows of orange trees in the grove. I had a lot of reasons to be thankful to the orchard. Not only did they grow the best oranges, the new owner was worth the trip.

I pulled Julie in for a proper kiss and sighed, not quite able to believe I'd found someone that enjoyed juice and oranges as much as I did. And I'd almost missed out on her because of my silly no competition rule. In hindsight, maybe I should've always been dating people in the business since they shared my passion for fruit.

With Julie in my arms, I was happier than I'd ever been. That was all a girl really needed. Love and freshly squeezed orange juice.

— The End —

I hope you liked this story about Lisa and Julie finding love. If you want to read more of this kind of cute romance, you should try out the rest of the Rainbow Central series. Try Love Is For Later, a friends-with-benefits to relationship romance or New Lease Of Love, an age-gap romance. Both books are set in Rainbow Central and you might recognise some familiar characters.

You can get Love Is For Later on most major retailers =>
https://books2read.com/loveisforlater

Or you can try Project Crush for free, where you'll see more of Erin => https://books2read.com/projectcrush

Signed Paperback & Merchandise:

You can find signed paperbacks, hardcovers, and merchandise based on my series (including stickers, magnets, face masks, and more!) via my website: www.arizonatape.com/shop

My website also has a selection of free stories and books that'll give you a taste of my other works: www.arizonatape.com/free

The Samantha Rain Mysteries

- Former detective, Samantha Rain, gets bitten by a hellhound puppy and drawn into a hidden Fae world where she meets the enchanting and sassy Lilith.
- An urban fantasy mystery series with an f/f romance.

The Griffin Sanctuary

- Animal lover and keeper-in-training, Charlotte, starts her internship at the

Griffin Sanctuary where she's tasked with caring for unicorns, griffins, and many other mythical animals on the verge of extinction.
- A modern fantasy series with an f/f romance.

The Forked Tail

- Grown bored of her job, glutton demon, Demi, bands together with lust demon and chef, Lana, to revolutionise the way demons eat sin.
- A fun modern fantasy series with an f/f romance.

The Afterlife Academy: Valkyrie

- Wind Child and Valkyrie student at the Afterlife Academy, Ylva, gets caught up in a sinister plan that could change the way afterlives work.
- A fantasy academy series with an f/f romance.

Queens Of The Underworld

- New Hades, Maia, finds the Underworld in chaos. Together with the current Persephone, it's up to them to bring order to the land of the dead.
- A fantasy series based on Greek mythology with an f/f romance.

Sapphire Bay Billionaires

- Romance stories about the elites and billionaires summering at the exclusive Sapphire Bay, living a life of extravagance, drama, and intrigue.
- A contemporary billionaire series with f/f romances, but each book can be read on its own.

My Winter Wolf

- On a quest to return a sacred relic, Akira meets a group of wolf-shifters that teach her the meaning of loyalty, love, and how to answer the call of the wolf.
- A fantasy series with an f/f romance.

Rainbow Central & The Romance Projects

- A collection of romance stories set in the LGBT bar, Rainbow Central bar, with various couples falling in love.
- A contemporary series with f/f romances.

The Twisted Princesses

- Twisted Princess Zafira meets her match in her brother's fiancée, Princess Jade, as they do whatever it takes to get the crown.
- A dark royal contemporary series with an f/f romance.
- Trigger warning: this series has dark themes and should be read with caution.

Her Vampire & My Own Human

- Vampire and scientist, Adrianna, meets who she believes is the last human, Heather. Stuck together, the two women discover they have more in common than they thought.
- A dystopian paranormal romance series with an f/f romance.
- Her Vampire is a remastered version of My Own Human. It loosely follows the

same storyline but has some fundamental differences.

Grimm's Dweller Trilogy

- Dweller of fictional worlds, Grisella, becomes fascinated by young writer, Wilhelm Grimm. Together, they create stories that stand the test of time.
- A fantasy series inspired by the fairytales of the Brothers Grimm.

Other Standalone Titles can be found on my website.

The Amethyst's Wand Shop Mysteries, co-written with Laura Greenwood

- Quirky witch and wandmaker, Amethyst, finally gets a chance to work with the Paranormal Police Department to solve all kinds of mysteries.
- An urban fantasy mystery series with an m/f romance.

The Vampire Detective, co-written with Laura Greenwood

- While solving various mysteries, Private Investigator and vampire, Lucy, discovers a nefarious plot that goes against everything she believes in.
- An urban fantasy mystery series with a polyamorous romance.

Purple Oasis, shared world with Laura Greenwood

- When their home collapses, a group of

witches and shifters are driven to find a
new place to settle. Along the way, they
test their magic, make friends for life, and
fall in love.
- A paranormal dystopian romance series
with f/f and m/f couples.

Twin Souls Trilogy, co-written with Laura Greenwood

- When vampire, Ayra, and dragon-shifter,
Tate, wake up in each other's bodies, they
discover their lives might not be
their own.
- A paranormal romance series with an f/f
and m/f couple.

Dragon Soul Series, co-written with Laura Greenwood

- Earth dragon and avid gamer, JJ, doesn't
believe in her arranged marriage. Earth
dragon and boxer, Holly, isn't ready to
leave the ring. Half-dragon, Marcus, looks
for a place to fit in. Three stories with
happy endings.
- A paranormal romance series with m/f
and f/f couples.

Renegade Dragons, co-written with Laura Greenwood

- Fire dragon, Lola, joins a team of gamers to win a tournament and finds victory and love.
- A paranormal romance series with a polyamorous romance that includes f/f and m/f pairings.

Aliens And Animals (co-written with Skye MacKinnon)

- Three alien sisters discover the joy of earth animals on their travels through space.
- An alien sci-fi series with f/f romances.

A creator at heart, Ari has always been in love with the idea of turning nothing into something. She wants to conquer the book world with stories that focus on inclusivity and diversity, writing what she likes to read. Whether it's adventure or romance, dragons and vampires, or princesses and students, there's something for everyone.

Born in China, raised in Belgium, and currently living in the United Kingdom with her girlfriend, Ari is a citizen of the world and loves discovering new cultures. Luckily, her crazy imagination lets her discover places she's never been to, meet people that don't exist, and talk to readers from all over the world.

FOLLOW THE AUTHOR

- Website: www.arizonatape.com

- Mailing List: www.arizonatape.com/subscribe
- Facebook Page: http://facebook.com/arizonatapeauthor
- Reader Group: http://facebook.com/groups/arizonatape
- Bookbub: http://www.bookbub.com/authors/arizona-tape
- Instagram: http://instagram.com/arizonatape